This book belongs to:

_____

_____

_____

First published 2020 by Walker Books Ltd
87 Vauxhall Walk, London SE11 5HJ

This edition published 2021

2 4 6 8 10 9 7 5 3 1

© 1990—2021 Lucy Cousins
Lucy Cousins font © 1990—2021 Lucy Cousins

The author's moral rights have been asserted

Maisy™. Maisy is a trademark of Walker Books Ltd, London

Printed in China

British Library Cataloguing in Publication Data:
a catalogue record for this book is
available from the British Library.

ISBN 978-1-4063-9962-2

www.walker.co.uk

Maisy
Gets a Pet

Lucy Cousins

WALKER BOOKS
AND SUBSIDIARIES
LONDON • BOSTON • SYDNEY • AUCKLAND

Maisy is visiting her friend Penguin today.

Penguin's cat has had
four kittens – 1, 2, 3, 4!

"The kittens are very small," explains Penguin, "so we need to take care and be gentle with them."

Maisy loves watching them all as they jump and play.

The little black kitten
climbs onto Maisy's lap.
When Maisy strokes her,
she gives a great big PURRR!

"Would you like to take a kitten
home?" Penguin asks.

Which kitten should Maisy choose?

The bouncy
ginger kitten
is very playful.

The stripy
kitten is
so brave!

The fluffy kitten is very soft.

But the little black kitten is Maisy's favourite.

Penguin gives Maisy a special carrier for the kitten. They put in newspaper, a blanket and some toys for the journey.

"I'm going to call her Little Black Cat!" says Maisy.

At first, Little Black Cat is scared of being somewhere new without her mummy.

Maisy waits very quietly.
Slowly, the kitten comes out
to see her new home.

Looking after
a pet is lots
of work!

Maisy feeds Little
Black Cat and gives
her fresh water
every day.

She cleans up
the litter tray.

And she gets
a scratching
post for the
kitten's claws.

Little Black Cat is growing very fast, so she needs lots of sleep. She naps in some very funny places!

Where is she now?

Maisy plays so many games with Little Black Cat.

They love to chase things and explore new places together.

It's good exercise
for Little
Black Cat ...

and for
Maisy,
too!

Soon it's time for Little Black Cat to visit Dr Furgood, the vet. They weigh her and give her special medicine to keep her healthy.

"What a lovely, friendly cat!" Dr Furgood says.

Maisy's friends come for a visit!

They're very
excited to meet
Maisy's new pet.

After a long day playing, it's time to go to bed.

Maisy gives Little Black Cat a big kiss and cuddle goodnight, and settles her down in a cosy basket to sleep...

Sweet dreams, Maisy.
Sweet dreams,
Little Black Cat.